Author's Note
The folk songs in this book are from my own collections and are the versions sung and played in the mountains of Tennessee.

To
The Taylors
of Camp Unaka

Table of Contents

1. The Outlanders 1
2. Meg Allen Does a Favor 8
3. A Real Friend 20
4. Grampy Has Visitors 32
5. Aunt Jody 44
6. The Wish Book Clothes 54

1
The Outlanders

Lizzie Holloway squinched up her toes against the slippery pebbles covering the stretch of road to the hotel grounds. A fairly unfitten' way it was for barefoot folk, she was thinking. No worriment, though, to the outlanders who wore shoes all the time.

But never mind, Lizzie thought to herself. Before the summer was over, she too would have a pair of shoes, shiny-bright as a blackbird's wing. And that wasn't all. She would have a new dress, blue or pink—she hadn't decided which—and a hat with a big bow to match. All were as yet a wish book dream. But Lizzie had high hopes that it was going to happen. She was doing her best to make her dream come true.

She pushed the raggedy bonnet brim and gave a glance at the posies packed in the splint basket slung across one arm. Better change to the other side of the road where it was less sunny, she thought.

It was another mile to the summer hotel; she'd better hurry along. The hotel lady would grumble again if the posy packs got wilted. She was mighty much particular about her table bouquets. Lizzie eyed the basket again. A pretty sight for certain it was now, with its marigolds, lady's fingers, touch-me-nots, old maids, spice pinks, and all the rest.

If the hotel lady should take all of these, the bright dream would come nearer. Lizzie's free hand felt in her pocket for her money bag. There were several dimes and nickels there—almost a dollar. She knew because she had counted her money the day before.

There had been a dollar and a half then. Part of it she had been obliged to spend at Cross Roads Store for a bottle of liniment to rub on Grampy's shoulder. Today he was better and able to plow Slow-Poke, the mule, in the late corn patch. Plowing made Grampy hungry. Lizzie must hurry back home and get his

Lizzie must hurry back home

dinner on time. The sunball over the mountain warned her that half the morning had already slipped away.

Lizzie was Grampy's housekeeper. He would often say she was a fairly good one for a gal-person her size and a wise-witted one for her years—she was ten, going on eleven—big enough, and old enough, to do some things very well.

She could make three kinds of bread: corn pone, hoecake, and dodgers. She could cook any mess in a kettle, from sallet to stirabout.

Hoecakes for dinner today, she planned. That kind of bread was quicker. She had left the bean pot simmering over a slow fire. For drink, there would be sassafras tea brewed till it was strengthy. Grampy would like two or three cups after his morning's work.

She had come now to the hotel grounds on the side of the mountain. The hotel itself, set back from the fence, was enough to dazzle the eye. Three stories high it was, painted yellow, with glass windows in the walls. She had never been inside the front yard fence. Folks with things to sell took them around to the kitchen.

As she was making the corner-turn, Lizzie heard someone say:

"Look, look. There she goes. It's Log Cabin Lizzie! She lives in that little old cabin that we passed yesterday." Lizzie glanced up, and her blue eyes flashed

Lizzie went on her way quietly

angrily as she saw a woman and a girl standing near the fence.

"Hush, she heard you!" the woman said.

Lizzie went on her way quietly, her head high, her face aflame under the sunbonnet. "Stuck-up outlanders," she thought, "with bigotty notions. Looking down on mountain folks, calling 'em names!" Then she stumbled against a hitching post, eyes tear-blinded. "Look-a-there now, will you!" she scolded herself. "Stumbling about like a lack-wit, certain-sure."

She squared her shoulders, wiped her eyes, set her old bonnet straight, and went through the back gate with her posies in order again.

When she came away, her big splint basket was empty. There were extra guests today, the hotel lady had said. That meant extra tables, of course, and more flowers for them. So Lizzie had sold the last one of her bouquets.

Her fingers felt for the money bag in her apron pocket, came out empty, and then felt again. The money bag was gone!

Gone! Where? There was no telling where. Maybe it was where she had stumbled against the hitching post. She must hurry back to see and to find her money bag. She hoped the two outlanders had gone clear away. She didn't want them to see her and have a chance to call her Log Cabin Lizzie again.

As she thought of it, her eyelids stung. But this was no time for crying. She mustn't waste time that way. She started out looking this way, looking that.

Then she saw the outlander woman and girl. They waved to her. One of them called to her. But Lizzie turned the other way and took to her heels, forgetting for the moment all about the money and scuttling away through the bushes like a varmint to its den.

2
Meg Allen Does a Favor

Hip-And-Hurrah, the old hound dog, came to the gate to meet her, cavorting about with his usual fuss to welcome her home.

"Yes," Lizzie said, with a careful look around, "you have been a good caretaker." He had kept Mammy Sow and her brood from the yard and the fowls from the posy beds. Lizzy gave Hip-and-Hurrah a pat and also a promise: "You shall have a hoecake for dinner today and a taste of stirabout, too."

"You shall have a hoecake for dinner today"

Lizzie looked at the cabin

Hip-and-Hurrah dashed on ahead to stretch himself in the wallow he had made for himself near the doorstep, from which he could watch the yard.

Lizzie stood stock-still in her tracks and looked at the cabin. "Little old cabin," the outlander girl had said. Was it little? She had never noticed that. It had seemed big a-plenty for her and Grampy, with its one pen room and a lean-to kitchen behind. Was it old? No doubt it was. Grampy had lived here all his life, and his pappy before him, too.

Little old cabin, no doubt, it looked to any outlander. "But that," thought Lizzie, "gave nobody any right to go misusing her name." Log Cabin Lizzie—it made her red-fire mad to think about it. Then she thought of her lost money bag. What an unlucky morning it had been.

Poor old Grampy looked so frazzled when he came in for dinner that Lizzie was worried.

"Grampy, you look downright dauncy," she said.

"No, no, honey," he answered her, "I'm just a little mullygrubby over the heat, I reckon. Don't pay any mind to me. What kind of luck did you have this morning peddling your posies?"

Lizzie managed a smile. "Good luck. I sold them all."

That was the truth. No need, she thought, to tell him about the piece of bad luck. It would make him feel mullygrubby certain-sure. At the table, she showed Grampy the money she had made from her flowers. The old man counted it over carefully in his gnarly hands.

"Why, it's over a dollar!" he cried. "A dollar and a dime it is, if I have not miscounted."

"That's right," Lizzie nodded.

"You'll soon have enough," Grampy said, "to buy that flock o' wish book clothes. You'll be fancy-fine for certain."

Grampy had heard tell about all these things time and time again.

Lizzie swallowed. She swallowed hard. "It'll take a little longer." She managed another smile as she passed a fresh hoecake to him.

Slinker, the cat, now slipped around to Grampy's side of the table and begged for a nibble, a trick he turned off three times every day. This time he got Grampy's share of the bread. The old man took but a nibble.

When Grampy was mincy about his food, he was dauncy, and no mistake.

She passed him a fresh cup of sassafras tea, red and strengthy. Grampy swigged it down with a smile. "A flavorsome brew," he said.

After dinner, he and Slow-Poke went back to the corn patch plowing. Lizzie busied herself about her own housework. First, she must ready-up the kitchen by washing up the dishes and sweeping the floor. The

Slinker, the cat, begged for a nibble

"Do please forgive me, Lizzie"

rest of the afternoon she planned to spend in her posy patch, weeding and hoeing.

She was hacking away at a jimsonweed that was crowding a lady's finger when all of a sudden she heard a step behind her. A voice said, "Hello!"

Lizzie turned around. Then her face flamed.

"Why—why—howdy," she stammered. She knew she was looking into the face of that outlander girl, the one she had seen that morning in the hotel yard. This was the girl who had called her Log Cabin Lizzie. Again she felt her face flame.

"I came—I came to bring you this," the outlander girl was saying, holding something out in her hand. "You lost this, didn't you?"

It was the little brown money bag.

Lizzie seized her treasure with a gladsome cry. Then she looked at the outlander girl.

"I'm mighty obliged to you."

This much she could say for manner's sake, and because she was truly thankful. Then she leaned on her hoe handle and looked the other way. "Let this outlander stand and stare as long as she likes," thought Lizzie. "A bigotty one in her store-boughten dress."

But the outlander girl was speaking again. "My name's Meg Allen. I'm staying with my Aunt Margaret up at the hotel."

Back went the old sunbonnet brim. "I'm Log Cabin Lizzie."

Blue eyes flashed into brown eyes and did not look away.

"Oh," Meg stammered, "you *did* hear me, then! I'm sorry. I'm ever so sorry. Do please forgive me, Lizzie, and let's be friends."

There were tears in the brown eyes now, but Lizzie's look was as steady and keen-sharp as her question in one word:

"Why?"

Meg smiled. "Oh, it would be such fun doing things together. I'm lonely up at the hotel. Aren't you lonely sometimes, down here?"

"Sometimes," Lizzie answered truthfully. "When Grampy's away," she added. "But you have your aunt, didn't you say, up there with you?"

"Yes," Meg nodded. "Aunt Margaret. She's like a mother to me, the only mother I've ever known. She's a lovely person, too, but she can't spend much time with me. She's busy writing stories. Maybe you've read some of them in books or magazines."

"No," Lizzie shook her head. Very few books or papers came to the cabin at the foot of Little Twin. "It would pleasure me to read one, I reckon," she added. "I'd rather read a story than eat sugar with a spoon!"

"You shall, I promise you!" Meg cried. "I'll bring you a nice new story, the one Aunt Margaret's writing now—just as soon as it's done. She always lets me read her stories first, to get my opinion." Meg's merry laugh

"Now I know you've forgiven me"

rang out. "It'll be lots of fun to share with you." She tossed back her curls. "And now, won't you show me your posies?"

Lizzie nodded her head. She couldn't do less for manner's sake, and Meg was due a favor, and a pretty good-sized favor, too, for returning the money bag. So she made Meg a posy pack, picking the prettiest blossoms and tying the stems together with honeysuckle vine. She handed it to her guest as a goodbye gift.

Meg threw her arms around Lizzie. "Now I know you've forgiven me, haven't you? And we're going to be good friends!"

3

A Real Friend

Grampy lay on a pallet bed in the corner of the cabin with old Hip-And-Hurrah curled up at his feet. A vinegar poultice was on his head to cool his fever, and a pine-tar plaster was on his back where he complained of a crick. Grampy had been sick for two days now, and he seemed to get no better, in spite of all the doctoring that Lizzie could do for him. She brewed a dozen different teas from herbs brought in

She brewed a dozen different teas

by the neighbors, who gave them along with much good will. But none of the herb teas worked a cure, though Grampy drank them all, much as he disliked the flavors. "Bittersome brews," he said, as he faithfully swallowed each dose.

Just now Grampy was taking a nap, and Lizzie was sitting near him, a leafy bough in her right hand to shoo away the flies. The wish book lay across her lap. She turned the pages softly, feasting her eyes on the pictures to pass the time away.

There was the hat with the ribbon bow, so pretty-fine and perky. How would it feel to wear a hat instead of a bonnet on her head? A few pages on was the frilly dress, as cheerful as a morning glory. *In blue or pink*, it said below. She thought she would take the blue. "Blue to match your eyes," Grampy had said, when she had sought his opinion.

Another page, and there was a pair of shiny patent leather shoes. She had been barefoot since 'way last spring. Shoes wore away with the winter, and as a rule, there were no new ones till winter came again. She'd never had a pair of shoes like these go-to-meeting shoes for Sunday. Her toes fairly itched to try them on.

Lizzie awoke from her dream to shoo a fly from Grampy's nose. Then she went on with her thinking, trying to do a sum by counting in her head. The hat would cost $1.00; the dress, $1.50. And the shoes—she looked again to be sure—$2.50. "Five dollars," she said

The wish book lay across her lap

The neighbors came to visit Grampy

to herself, after a few minutes. She had a good bit of money to earn yet.

Grampy groaned and opened his eyes. He didn't seem any better, Lizzie thought. She got up to change the poultice on his head.

The next day he was a good deal worse, and Lizzie sent for the doctor five miles away in Far Beyant. He examined Grampy and said, "Too much work. He must take a rest and eat more nourishing food. I'll leave him a bottle of tonic, too."

He threw away the vinegar poultice, as well as the pine-tar plaster, and got Grampy up from his pallet into his four-poster bed.

Lizzie got out her money bag to pay the doctor. He charged her less than his usual fee, but still it took all she had.

"But I don't care. I don't care a *mite* to give up the money," thought Lizzie. She put her wish book dreams in the back of her head.

The neighbors were very good these days. They came to visit Grampy, and none came empty-handed. There were many gifts of food: chicken broth, new-laid eggs, a loaf of bread, a piece of honey in the comb, and many more nice things.

Lizzie was glad and grateful too, to have such friendly favors. It would have been hard, sure-enough, to manage all by herself. As it was, she had to use her wits and will to keep things going, doing her chores in patchwork fashion as she got the chance. A neighbor who sat with Grampy an hour gave her much time for hoeing in the garden behind her house or in her posy beds.

She loaned the mule Slow-Poke around in return for the plowing which she couldn't do herself. She saved three dozen eggs and sent by a neighbor to Far Beyant for another bottle of tonic. Eggs brought a better price there than they did at Cross Roads Store.

As for her peddling job, she thought she would have to give it up till Grampy was much better. The wish book dream in the back of her head she had given up for good.

Here came Meg, the outlander girl, one day while Lizzie was hoeing her posies.

"Whatever has happened? I've watched for you all these days!" she said. "We miss your flowers on the tables, too."

Lizzie explained about Grampy.

"Oh, I hadn't heard! I'm so sorry. That's too bad. I wish—can't I do something to help?"

"I reckon not," replied Lizzie. If this outlander should try to hoe, she wouldn't know a posy from a weed! Not unless it was blooming anyhow. Lizzie smiled under her bonnet.

But now Meg Allen was clapping her hands.

"Listen, oh listen, Lizzie! Just this minute a grand idea has popped right up in my head. Let me peddle

She saved the eggs

She brought Lizzie a new chapter of the story

your flowers for you. Oh, I should love to do it! Fun for me and money for you. What do you say?"

"Oh," said Lizzie, "that's kind of you, mighty kind and thoughty, but I couldn't be beholden for such a favor as that."

"What's beholden?" Meg asked in a puzzled manner.

"Taking favors you can't repay."

Meg Allen laughed. "Oh, the favors would be all mine! By the way, I brought you that story. Read it whenever you have the time. I'll be back and get it someday before long." She turned to go.

"Wait a minute," Lizzie told her. "I want to give you a thank-gift." She made Meg a big bouquet.

"I do thank you mighty-much," she said, "for wanting to help me, but it's not such a *big* job, after all, and I can manage by myself."

Meg Allen nodded. "Thank you for the flowers. Oh, they are lovely!" A strange little wishful look passed across her face.

"Come back," Lizzie bade the outlander girl.

"Yes, I will," Meg promised. "I'll bring you another story soon. Aunt Margaret's writing a book, a story for every chapter. And I'm going to let you read every one!"

"Much obliged," Lizzie said.

After this, she began to feel more friendly toward Meg Allen. How could she help it when Meg seemed so friendly-wise to her? Outlander she might be, but she was no bigotty person, even if she did wear a store-boughten dress and shoes.

Almost every time she came, she brought Lizzie a new chapter of the story fresh from her Aunt Margaret's pen. They were all about the pioneers who had settled the mountain. The title of the book was to be *Legends of Little Twin Mountain*.

"How does she learn so many things about the mountain people?" Lizzie wondered. She questioned Meg the very next time she came.

Meg laughed. "Aunt Margaret gets her stories from right around here. It's a funny sort of game hunting them up, like hide-and-seek. She goes all over the mountain. Sometimes people will talk to her. Sometimes they won't. Once she heard someone say, 'There goes the outlander woman,' and whoever it was went away just as quickly as she could."

Lizzie's face went all aflame. Why, it might have been herself! A new notion came into her head. Maybe outlander people didn't like to be called any such name. Outlander. Yes, it might sound almost as unfriendly as Log Cabin Lizzie.

"I reckon," she said to Meg, "sometimes folks don't understand other folkses' feelings." Another notion came to mind. "Maybe if your aunt came here someday, Grampy could tell her a tale or two. Grampy's a fine tale-teller. And he might tune up some time and play her a fiddle-jig, too!"

Meg clapped her hands. "Oh, that will be fun! And Auntie will be delighted."

That day Lizzie gave Meg an extra big posy pack.

4
Grampy Has Visitors

Grampy was still in bed, but he was a far sight better. He could even sit up now for a spell with pillows behind his head.

Lizzie could leave him alone sometimes with only Hip-and-Hurrah and Slinker there in the cabin to keep him company.

One day he called for his fiddle box, and Lizzie was tickled to hear him strike up his favorite tune about the groundhog—*The Whistle Pig.*

One day he called for his fiddle box

Grampy was better, certain-sure. No doubt about it!

All of a sudden he began to sing, and Lizzie, who liked the old song, too, began to sing with him.

THE WHISTLE PIG

"Come on, hurry, and let's go down,
Come on, hurry, and let's go down,
Let's catch a whistle pig in the ground,
Come a-ring-ding, dingle-ing-a-di-de-oh!

"Up came Pappy from the plow,
Up came Pappy from the plow,
Catch that whistle pig, catch him now,
Come a-ring-ding, dingle-ing-a-di-de-oh!

"Up came Mammy from the spring,
Up came Mammy from the spring,
Whistle-pig grease all over her chin,
Come a-ring-ding, dingle-ing-a-di-de-oh!"

Lizzie was happy again. Bad luck seemed to be behind them with the passing of Grampy's sickness. Lizzie thought she would never complain of any misfortune less than this.

Then something else happened.

One night a stormy wind blew up Darksome Hollow, tearing half a dozen roof boards off. Worst of

A downpour of rain followed

all, a downpour of rain followed, part of it landing on poor Grampy's bed.

"The Great Forever-And-Forevermore!" he began yelling. "It's another flood. And this log cabin ain't Noah's Ark!"

Lizzie took a towel to Grampy's wet head. Then she made a tent out of bed covers to keep the rest of the rain off. Daylight showed a hole in the roof that a body could sling a cat through without hitting the edges.

"What a happenstance!" Grampy growled. "And me lying helpless here!"

"Don't get mullygrubby," Lizzie begged. "Don't be dolesome, Grampy, for I've a notion in my head I can fix the roof myself."

"The Great Forever-And-Forevermore! You'll break your neck for certain iffen you was to try such a trick as that!" Grampy said.

"Don't feel flustery," Lizzie laughed. "No need to be a-feared, Grampy. I can climb any tree on Little Twin, and I can climb up there and fix that roof. And I can hammer a nail because you taught me."

Grampy grinned. "Well, maybe you can. You're a right sharp-witted young'un, I'll say that much, though I hadn't ought to praise you to your face."

Lizzie was sitting astride the ridgepole when she looked up the mountain and saw Meg Allen and a woman behind her coming down Little Twin Trail.

"Grampy!" she called down through the roof hole that was still half-uncovered. "Here comes company to see you."

"Who is it?" Grampy yelled. "Kinfolk or neighbors?"

"It's Meg and her aunt," said Lizzy. "Her aunt is the writing woman that I was telling you about."

"The Great Forever-And-Forevermore!" cried Grampy. "I wish that outlander woman could have picked another day to traipse down here! What'll she think when she sees things in such an upscuddle?"

Lizzie laughed. "She'll understand when she sees this hole in the roof. Don't feel fussy-fied, Grampy. Hurry and comb your whiskers. The company's got to the foot-log— Now they're crossing Kettle Creek."

She was climbing down from her high perch now in a hip-and-hurry and barely had time to meet the company in a mannerly way.

"Come in and take a chair. Make yourself at home," she said shyly.

"Come in and shut one eye on your whereabouts," Grampy said.

"Never mind, never mind," smiled Miss Allen. "I can see the trouble that you had. It reminds me of the time when a cyclone once came our way and took off the roof, and a rain came right on the heels of it."

She went on telling the story. A very good story it was, Lizzie thought.

"She'll understand when she sees this hole"

When it was done, Grampy cried: "That reminds me of a tale that happened on Twin Mountain years and years ago, before I was born. I heard it from my pappy, and he heard it from *his* pappy, and so on. It goes back clear to pioneer days!"

"May I use my notebook and pencil?" the writing woman asked. "Now, I am ready. Do please go on."

Grampy nodded and began his yarn.

"Lew Owens was a long hunter. A long hunter was one who went on lengthy hunting trips from several months to a year. He'd traipse around in the wilderness, tracking and trapping the fur-bearing critters that were then in Tennessee. That was a certain-sure way of making money, if a hunter had fair luck.

"Lew Owens was said to be one of the best of the hunting tribe. Winter after winter, he'd strike out for the wilderness, and his neighbors wouldn't see him again till spring, or maybe summer. But he'd always come back richer than he went away. Finally, he moved his wife and seven children clear away from the settlement on Little Twin. Some of the neighbors asked him where he was going.

"'Away out yonder,' was all Lew Owens would tell.

"Living in the wilderness had made him a wild critter. More like a varmint than a man, you might say.

"Years passed. My great-grandfather with some other surveyors went through the Great Smokies to lay the state line. They came across Lew Owens, his wife, and thirteen young'uns. Yes, his family was bigger by this time. They were living on a mountainside in a roofless cabin. The wind wouldn't let the roof stay on, Lew Owens explained. But they got along right well, he said, till wet weather, and then they took shelter in a hollow tree."

The writing woman looked up, and her eyes twinkled. "That must have been a very big tree," she said.

Grampy grinned back at her. "It wasn't one tree," he told her. "Lew Owens' folks all had a tree apiece!"

They all laughed. "What a good story—with a perfect ending. Thank you so much," the writing woman said. "It will make a chapter in my book, *Legends of Little Twin Mountain*. Someday I'll send you a copy, with this story appearing under your name."

Grampy grinned. Then he chuckled outright. "Think of that now!" he shouted. "The Great Forever-And-Forevermore! I'll never feel the same after seeing my name in print. A wonderly thing to happen. I'll be the proud-fullest person on this side of the Little Twin."

Lizzie leaned over and whispered to Meg, "Grampy's tickled to pieces. He looks as chirky as if he had taken ten doses of medicine!"

The night rain and the morning sun had freshened all the flowers, so Lizzie took her visitors into the posy patch just before they started home. She gathered two big bouquets, one apiece for them.

She told them: "You-all hurry back," in a mannerly fashion. After they had gone away, she went on with her job. That roof hole must be well patched against squally weather. No telling how soon a storm would blow up the hollow again.

While she was hammering away, she heard Grampy's old fiddle strike up a rollicking tune. It was *The Whistle Pig* again.

She had heard him promise the visitors to play that fiddle-jig for them sometime, maybe next time they came.

5
Aunt Jody

Lizzie and Grampy were sitting in the doorway of their cabin when all of a sudden, and at the same time, what should they see?

Here came Aunt Jody Hollaway, footing it down the mountain, clear from the other side, a lengthy far way. Aunt Jody was well-laden with a hip-poke and also a shoulder pack. The hip-poke, which was the smaller of the two, contained all the clothing she would need for

Here came Aunt Jody Hollaway

She showed them all the herbs

a nice long visit. Then she opened the shoulder-pack and showed them all the herbs she had brought—dozens and dozens of bunches.

As she pointed them out, she took time to explain: "Heal-all for nervousness. Ragweed for dropsy. Pennyroyal for coughs and colds. Tansy for bee stings. Spice-wood for headache. Bloodroot for weak trembles. Thorn apple for boils."

Aunt Jody knew the name of every herb that was in the bag.

"But what are you a-going to do with such a lot?" asked Lizzy.

"Make 'em into medicine sooner or later," Aunt Jody said, "just as they happen to be needed. I tote my herb pack along with me whenever I visit the sick."

"The Great Forever-And-Forevermore!" said Grampy. "There's nobody sick around here," and he winked at Lizzie. "I was dauncy for a spell, but now I am on the mend. Reckon you got here a mite late to doctor me," he added slyly. Another wink at Lizzie, and she winked back to show him she understood. Grampy didn't like herb tea, as Lizzie well remembered.

Aunt Jody gave him a long, keen look. "We'll see. We'll see," she said.

She hung her hip-poke on a wall peg, her shoulder-pack just below.

"Now that I'm here," she told them, "I might as well stay a spell."

"Make yourself at home," said Grampy in a mannerly fashion, but he was a mite distrustful as Lizzie could tell.

Aunt Jody said no more about doctoring Grampy, and the only tea he was given to drink was sassafras tea with short sweetening in it. Short sweetening is sugar. Long sweetening, or molasses, was the kind they usually had. Short sweetening was, as a rule, saved for company.

Aunt Jody promised to make a stack cake for their very next meal. "Stack cake and sassafras tea go well together," she said. "I'll make you a good one."

She kept her word. She showed Lizzie how to make the cake, and to help her remember, she taught her this very old recipe rhyme:

"Three double-handfuls and one more of flour,
Two cups o' sweet milk, one cup o' sour.
A thumb pinch of soda, make no mistake,
And one cup o' sorghum to make up the cake."

"Mighty obliged to you, Aunt Jody," said Lizzie. "Sometime I aim to try it all by myself."

She was liking Aunt Jody more and more. A wise-witted woman she was, and kind-hearted, too, Lizzie was finding out.

Lizzie began to nod at last

That night, after supper was cleared away, they all sat outside the cabin and sang ballads to the tunes that Aunt Jody suggested. They sang these old songs all by heart. Some of them were rather lengthy, telling tales of long ago and far away.

Lizzie began to nod at last over the tune of an old mountain ballad—*True Love's Farewell*. The tune, and the words as well, sang themselves into a dream which took her beyond the cabin into another world.

TRUE LOVE'S FAREWELL

Oh, who will shoe my little feet, feet, feet?
Oh, who will shoe my little feet, feet, feet?
Oh, who will shoe my little feet,
When I am in a distant land?

Oh, who will glove my little hands, hands, hands?
Oh, who will glove my little hands, hands, hands?
Oh, who will glove my little hands,
When I am in a distant land?

Oh, who will kiss my rosy lips, lips, lips?
Oh, who will kiss my rosy lips, lips, lips?
Oh, who will kiss my rosy lips,
When I am in a distant land?

Old Hip-And-Hurrah nuzzled her face, and Lizzie awoke all of a sudden to find herself peering through the shadows of the yard.

The sweet smell of pinks and pretty-by-nights drifted about her. Lizzie sniffed in sleepily, and a thought came into her head: Now she was free again to peddle posies. There would be money again in the little brown bag. Maybe there would be enough before the summer was over to buy the hat and dress to match and the pair of patent leather shoes.

6
The Wish Book Clothes

Lizzie was climbing Little Twin Trail in the cool of early morning. She had risen at dawn light to get a good start. Posies gathered dewy-damp kept a lot longer than the ones picked in the heat of the day.

As she was taking the turn that led to the hotel kitchen, somebody called from a window, "Wait, Lizzie!"

It was Meg. A moment later, she dashed from the door. "Oh, I'm glad I saw you in time to tell you the

Somebody called from a window, "Wait, Lizzie!"

"There's about five dollars there, I think"

secret myself, though I hate to give it away before I had more money for you!"

Lizzie's face was puzzled. "Secret? Money?" she stammered. "Whatever do you mean?"

Meg laughed. "You could never guess! I sold the bouquets you gave me to the hotel for the dining room. And here's the money for you."

From a pocket, she took out a purse and handed it to Lizzie. "There's about five dollars there, I think."

"Oh—oh!" Lizzie gasped. It made her dizzy to think of it. Such luck all of a sudden! What a surprise! And what a fine joke Meg had played on her. Lizzie laughed.

"You don't mind?" Meg's eyes twinkled.

Lizzie's twinkled back. "Reckon I don't, though I can't deny that I am beholden to you for a favor. And that's a secret *you* could never guess!"

"Tell me, oh, tell me, please!" cried Meg, with her face all glowing like a pink posy. "I just can't wait to hear!"

"Well, I'll tell you then," said Lizzie. "I was saving up my money to buy me a flock of wish book clothes. That's what I aimed to do. Then Grampy took down sick, you know, and I had to pay the doctor man out o' what I saved up. Then the peddling stopped, too. But now—" She looked down at the purse. "Why, I can take this money and buy a blue dress with a hat to match and a pair o' patent leather shoes!"

"Oh!" cried Meg as she hugged her friend. "I'm so happy for you! I declare, Lizzie, I believe I'm almost as glad as you are. Do please order your wish book things at once, won't you? I want to see you all dressed up before we go away."

"Away? You're going away? When?" stammered Lizzie.

Meg nodded. "Yes, we plan to go back home sometime next week. To Johnson City. Oh, Lizzie, I wish—I *wish* that you could go home with us! You'd like that, too, I know you would, and I don't see why you can't."

"Grampy mightn't want to let me go so far away," said Lizzie. "And the new clothes might not get here in time to wear on the trip."

Meg laughed. "I don't believe that those are very good excuses! Let's see if we can't manage things anyway."

The two girls hurried back over Little Twin Trail to Grampy. They wanted to talk the big plan over with him.

He listened to them without interruption, nodding his head and combing his long beard with his fingers.

"A pretty fine notion, certain-sure. That's what I think," he said.

"Certain-sure it is!" echoed Aunt Jody, who had come into the cabin just in time to hear what they were talking about. "It's as good a chance for a visit

Lizzie ordered the wish book clothes

Lizzie was standing there waiting for him

as you are likely to have for many a year. Here I am, and here I stay to housekeep for you till you come home again."

One worry was cleared away, anyhow. Lizzie sat down while Meg was there to help her and ordered the wish book clothes. The letter went off the next day.

"Whoa, Beck! Whoa, Heck!" Uncle Bildad Cooley stopped the mail wagon at the place where Kettle Creek Trail turns into the big wagon road. He had just caught sight of Lizzie standing there waiting for him. She had on a bright blue dress, a hat with a big blue bow, and new shoes, shiny and slick. It was no riddle for Uncle Bildad to guess that here was a passenger.

"Howdy, Lizzie!" he hailed her. "Reckon you are aiming to go on a journey-jaunt today."

"Yes," she answered, "I am going to make a visit."

"Do tell!" cried the mailman. And again he cried, "Do tell!" as he helped her up into the wagon.

"You'll have company as soon as we stop at the hotel. One lady person and a little gal going to Johnson City. They have to catch the noon train in Far Beyant."

"So do I," Lizzie said, smiling sideways at him. Then, glancing down at her patent leather shoes, she added, "This isn't a *traipsing* trip, Uncle Bildad. I'm going to travel with those hotel folks, and I'm going to visit them. They're my friends!"

"Do tell! Do tell!" Uncle Bildad muttered. "Get on, Beck! Get on, Heck!"

His mail wagon rolled on.

Around the turn stood the summer hotel. Meg and her aunt were sitting on the big front porch with their bags piled all about.

"Got to stop here and load up, I guess," said Uncle Bildad as he got down. "Will you hold the lines till I get back?"

"Of course," agreed Lizzie, but she was paying little attention to the horses. Meg and her aunt were already hurrying over.

"How pretty you look!" exclaimed Meg. "Just like a picture in the wish book, doesn't she, Aunt Margaret?"

"Yes, she does indeed," said Meg's aunt, dividing her attention between Lizzie and the bags.

At last everything and everybody was tucked safely in.

"All off!" cried Uncle Bildad. "Here we go. Get on, Beck! Get on, Heck!"

The mail wagon started again.

More Books from The Good and the Beautiful Library!

Race for the Prairie
by Aileen Fisher

Melissa Across the Fence
by Augusta Huiell Seaman

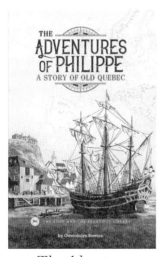

*The Adventures
of Philippe*
by Gwendolyn Bowers

Slave Boy in Judea
by Josephine Sanger Lau

www.thegoodandthebeautiful.com

SUSIE

by May Justus

First published in 1947

This unabridged version has updated grammar and spelling.

© 2019 Jenny Phillips

www.thegoodandthebeautiful.com

Cover illustration by

Ecaterina Leascenco and Christine Chisholm

Cover design by Elle Staples

Illustrations by Christine Chisholm

To Miss Bessie
*whose heart and house are
open to all who need her*

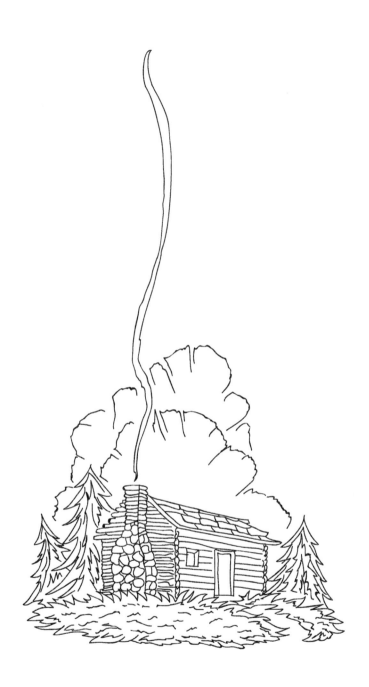

Susie, Joe, and Jim

Author's Note

The folksongs in this book are from my own collection and are taken from the version in which they were given to me.

Table of Contents

Chapter 1 1

Chapter 2 9

Chapter 3 18

Chapter 4 26

Chapter 5 39

Susie

Chapter 1

The sunball was dropping low in the pocket of No-End Hollow as Susie Linders shouldered her herb sack and started up the homeward trail. Although the sack was nearly full, it wasn't heavy. Over the other shoulder, she toted a grubbing hoe.

She had been grub-hunting all afternoon for the dozen different kinds of herbs Mammy needed to make a certain tea. A brown, bittersome brew it was, for Mammy made it strong. She declared the more herbs that went into it, the better it would be.

Mammy was a wise-witted woman in her knowledge of mountain herbs. She could neither read nor write; in fact, she had never been to school. But she had sense a-plenty. Her ways of curing sick folks would have filled a big-sized book. She was doctoring somebody all the time, either her own folks or the neighbors.

"There's hardly a thing that grows," she would say, "but what is good for something. There's pennyroyal—that's good for colds." The twins, Joe and Jim, who were forever having snuffles, got their share of this.

Mammy was a wise-witted woman

"There's no better tonic than sourwood sprouts, leaves, twigs, and roots boiled together." Pappy always groaned when she made him take a dose of it.

"And elderberry tea is mighty good when a young'un gets the colic." The baby got a good deal of this.

As for Susie, she was seldom sick. If she ever felt a little dauncy, she usually thought it best not to mention it.

One thing, however, Susie couldn't escape, and that was Mammy's yearly dosing with the medicine which she called Spring Tea. It came along as regularly as corn planting, wake robins in the hollow, and dandelion greens. Spring Tea was good for folks, even if they weren't ailing.

"It makes sick folks well and well ones better," Mammy would say.

As a rule, Mammy liked to do her own herb-hunting, with some of the young ones

She found a cliff starred over with windflowers

tagging along, mostly for company. But for the last few days, the baby had been a mite puny and fretful. The twins, of course, couldn't be trusted to hunt herbs. They'd slip off with Lazybones, their dog, and go hunting some wild varmint.

Susie shifted the sack and hoe to opposite shoulders. It would be harder, she thought, to drink her share of Spring Tea than it had been to gather the herbs for its brewing.

On the whole, though, the afternoon had passed most pleasantly. She had found a batch of spring beauties 'way down in the hollow, a clump of bloodroot blossoms with petals as white as snow, and a cliff starred over with windflowers. She had a few of these in her bonnet swinging down her back from the knotted strings. These would look nice in a little

Susie liked to romp and run

gourd bowl in the middle of the kitchen table, along about suppertime.

"Pretty as a posy—" She liked that old saying. She often wished she looked a little like some posy herself. But she couldn't, not with her straight black hair and skin like saddle leather. If she'd roll her hair on slim cornstalks or wear a bonnet on her head, she might improve a little. Some girls did. But all this was a sight of trouble for one who liked to romp and run and feel as free as the wind.

Chapter 2

As Susie neared her cabin home, the twins ran down the trail to meet her, with Lazybones ducking and dodging between their legs.

"Guess what!" cried Joe, nearly out of breath.

"Guess what!" Jim echoed.

The boys were like two chestnuts in one burr. It was hard to tell them apart. Both had blue eyes and curly brown hair, and they took after Pappy. But Joe had some hair that stuck up, while Jim did not. They were nine years old. Susie was ten, but they were as big as she was.

"Guess what!" cried Joe again, and Jim added, "Guess. Guess what!"

Susie handed Joe the herb sack and Jim the grubbing hoe.

"Some trick you are trying to play on me, like as not!" She gave her brothers a keen look. She knew those boys. It tickled them to pieces to play a joke on her.

But now they both turned solemn-like and sobersome all of a sudden.

"It's not a trick!" Joe went on, wagging his head back and forth.

"It's not," said Jim. "It's a sure-enough surprise. It is for certain."

"Certain-*sure*?" asked Susie.

They were nine years old

"Yes," said Joe.

"All right, I'll guess," agreed Susie. "I'll guess that it's something in a pot, something for supper—maybe chicken and dumplings. Mammy's been threatening to kill the old Plymouth Rock hen."

Joe gave Jim a wondering look, and Jim looked back at his brother.

Susie knew she had guessed right. "Well, now, what about that?" She started to laugh but stopped short when Joe turned to speak to her.

"You didn't guess all the surprise, just about half of it!"

"Just about half," added Jim.

"Oh," said Susie. "Half is about all I can do. You'll have to tell the rest."

The boys looked at each other, then said in one breath: "Company!"

The twins raced on before her

"Company," Susie echoed. "Tell me who," she begged them.

They might have tease-talked a spell with her, trying to make her guess, if they hadn't that moment come in sight of the double-pen cabin sitting like a brooding bird in a turn of the mountain trail. Susie caught sight of a two-wheeled cart propped against one wall of the cabin.

"Why, it's Step-Along, the peddler man!" she said.

"He's going to stay for supper," said Joc.

"He's to stay all night," Jim added.

"Goody, oh, goody!" Susie said. "Then he'll show us all his things!"

"Whoopee. Whoop!" The twins shouted. They raced on before her, their voices mingling with the barks of the hound dog, Lazybones.

A fine, flavorsome smell came out of the kitchen door as they entered.

"Chicken and dumplings!" Susie thought. She'd guessed right about that old hen.

Pappy and the peddler man were smoking their pipes in a corner.

"Howdy, Sissy," Step-Along said as Susie came up. He got up in a mannerly way and shook hands with her. "I hear tell you're an herb woman like your ma."

He glanced at the poke of herbs which the boys had dumped into another corner. It had come untied, and a pile of roots had spilled upon the floor.

Susie started to gather them up when Mammy called her to come and help with supper in the back part of the room.

"Get a jar of huckleberry jam," Mammy said, "from the top shelf in the cupboard. I've sent

"I've sent the boys to get the milk and butter"

the boys to get the milk and butter at the spring. I've made up a batch of biscuit bread. With the chicken and dumplings, we'll have a fairly-fine supper." She nodded her head happily.

Susie nodded her head too. "We will, for a fact, I reckon."

Chapter 3

Susie caught an earful of talk now and then from the men seated in the corner. They were trading tall tales back and forth, laughing between their stories.

The Linders had little company—the preacher, the peddler man, and some kin from Yon Side now and then. They had no near

Susie hurried back and forth setting food on the table

neighbors, and those who lived mountain miles away did little visiting.

Susie hurried back and forth setting food on the table. As soon as supper was over, there would be music and songs. Pappy would play his old red fiddle. Mammy would lead them in ballad singing. They would have a gladsome time.

By and by, so as not to seem in a hurry, Step-Along would open his peddler's pack. That was always a sight to behold, a fancy-fine sight, for certain. All the family liked to look at these brought-on knick-knacks, even though they had no money to buy any of the pretties. Better than a new wish book was the peddler's pack.

Mammy opened the kitchen door and gave a whoop-and-holler for the boys who had lingered overlong on their errand.

The hound dog had scented some varmint

They came in with a tale to tell. The hound dog had scented some varmint in a hole of the creek bank and had tried to follow it.

"Reckon you boys did the same thing by the looks of your wet clothes," said Mammy. "Don't know which is more bedraggled, Lazybones or you twins. I'll dose you both with hot herb tea. I'll brew it right after supper to keep you from catching cold."

Mammy did not see the wry faces of the twins. A few minutes later, she gave the call: "Come set your feet under the table." This was her usual invitation when a meal was in its place.

Susie helped to serve the food, passing around the table, paying special attention to their guest. Step-Along bragged about everything, speaking in praiseful fashion of the chicken and dumplings, the jam, and the biscuit bread.

"Wish I could board with you folks awhile. Reckon I'd soon get as hefty as Pat Farley on Yon Side. They say he weighs three hundred pounds!"

Just then he sneezed, and Mammy pushed the salt gourd across the table.

"Throw a pinch over your shoulder," she cried, "to keep bad luck from you!"

Step-Along did as she said, for he thought, as well as all the others, that it is bad luck to sneeze at the table before a meal is over.

"I'm mighty afeared," he said, "that the bad luck's already happened. I'm afeared I caught myself a cold. I waded through the creek back yonder a mile or so where the old foot-log was missing." And he gave another loud, "Ker-choo!"

Mammy got up. "I'll get that herb pot on in a hip-and-hurry. I'll make a brewing of good herb tea for you. And the boys, too," she added.

"I waded through the creek back yonder"

"Give him my share, Mammy," Joe spoke up. "I don't believe I need it."

"And give him mine," Jimmy nodded hopefully. "I feel all right. I do."

"There'll be enough for all," Mammy said. "No use in taking chances. It'll keep you well, or make you well, as I always say."

Susie helped Mammy sort the herbs and get them ready for the kettle which was set to steam away on the high chimney hook. Spicewood, boneset, pennyroyal shoots, bark from slippery elm, wintergreen spears, heart leaves, and several others, too—all went into the kettle.

Soon the sharp tang of the brew filled the cabin room.

"It's a strong smell," said the peddler. "That tea ought to cure a cold in no time."

"It ought to cure mad-dog bite, as bad as it tastes," Pappy said with a grin and a wink in the boys' direction.

Joe and Jim uttered a groan in one long breath.

Chapter 4

Susie thought it was high time for something cheerful to happen. She wished Step-Along would think of opening his pack. Maybe if she reminded him, made him think about it— "It's a good thing you didn't take your load clear on to Far Beyant tonight," she said, eyeing the big sack dumped in a corner. "You might have to wade another creek by happenstance."

The notion worked. Step-Along got up and brought forth his bag of treasures. "Now's the time I was waiting for to show you my wares. Yes-sir-ee, I had planned to do so right after supper. Come one—come all, and take a look at the fancy-fine things I have here!"

He opened the sack in front of the hearth, and out poured a colorful jumble, spilling into a pile on the clean floor. There were rolls of bright ribbon, gay neckties, rainbow-hued handkerchiefs, scissors, pocket knives, bead necklaces, papers of needles and pins, a baby's shiny rattler, and many other things.

The Linders stood around and stared.

"A sight to behold!" said Pappy.

"A sight, sure-enough it is," Mammy agreed.

He opened the sack in front of the hearth

The children said nothing at all. They were all spellbound and tongue-tied with the wonderful show spread there before them.

Perhaps Step-Along's keen eyes saw what each one was looking upon. He began to call attention to the merits of this and that and to praise his wares.

"Look-a-here, boys. See these jackknives? Genuine bone handles. Three fine blades apiece and sharp enough to split a hair!" He handed the boys the knives.

"Now, Sissy, look-a-here—a red ribbon for your pigtails when you dress up for Sunday. You'll look pretty as a posy then. I vow and declare you will." He put the ribbon into Susie's hands, then began to show Pappy half a dozen neckties all at once.

Before Mammy's eyes he spread a piece of dress goods and lace for trimming, as well as some pretty buttons.

"A red ribbon for your pigtails"

The Linders looked and looked and looked till their eyes were fairly filled. They knew these treasures could not be theirs, not even the cheapest of them. There was never much money on hand, and none this time of year. Winter was always a long, lean time for the folks on Little Twin Mountain, and the Linders family was among the poorest of the poor. For food, they had the things they had stored in the loft room and cellar. Clothes were patched till they wore clear out and so were the shoes. Sometimes Pappy sold a varmint skin, using the money to buy soda, salt, or tobacco. Or Mammy might sell a few eggs now and then.

Of course, they all knew they couldn't buy any of the peddler's stuff.

It was Pappy who spoke for them. "Reckon we'll wait till another time to buy anything from you. But we're mighty-much obliged to have a look at all your fine truck, Peddler. It's a sight to behold, certain-sure!"

The boys laid down the jackknives. Susie put down the red ribbon. Their sighs went up as one sound.

Just then the night wind blew a puff of air down the chimney and set them all to coughing.

"A sign of bad weather," Pappy said.

Now a loud "Ker-choo" from Step-Along reminded Mammy of her herb pot. She drew in a whiff of the bittersome smell. "Bad weather means more colds. I'd better dose all of you, come bedtime."

"Ooh—ooh!" Joe grunted.

"Ooh—ooh!" Jim groaned.

Susie sighed sadly.

Then all of a sudden a notion popped into Susie's head. She turned with a smile to Pappy and said: "Play us a fiddle tune."

Faces brightened in the pine-knot fire that lit the cabin room.

"Yes, yes," the chorus went up. They all liked Susie's notion.

Step-Along began to clap his hands in time. "Fiddle away!" he cried. "There's nothing I like better than—ker-choo! Oh, I'm afraid that cold is coming along!"

"The herb tea's about ready," Mammy said, sniffing the smell from the kettle. "It'll be fitten for you about bedtime."

Pappy had taken his fiddle down from its wall peg. "I'll play if somebody will sing."

The two boys shook their heads. They wouldn't sing before company. They were too timid.

"I've got to sample that tea right now. Excuse me," Mammy said.

Pappy looked over the fiddle bridge and winked at Susie. "What about *Lazy Lady*?"

Susie nodded her head.

Fiddle-dee-dee! went the fiddle bow. Susie started to sing:

Fiddle-dee-dee! went the fiddle bow

LAZY LADY

"Do, do, pity my case, ladies in the garden,
My bread to bake when I get home, ladies
   in the garden.

"Do, do, pity my case, ladies in the garden,
My clothes to wash when I get home, ladies
   in the garden.

"Do, do, pity my case, ladies in the garden,
My floors to scrub when I get home, ladies
   in the garden.

"Do, do, pity my case, ladies in the garden,
My flock to feed when I get
home, ladies
   in the garden.

"Do, do, pity my case, ladies in the garden,
My cow to milk when I get home—"

"Ker-choo!" sneezed the peddler so loudly that the rafters seemed to shake.

Pappy nearly dropped his fiddle, while Susie stopped before her song quite came to an end.

Just then the boys began to sneeze. Each promptly pinched the end of his nose, but it was too late to stop.

"Ker-choo!" went Joe's sneeze.

"Ker-choo!" went Jim's echo.

"Come one, come all! This herb tea's good and ready!" Mammy cried cheerfully.

Willy-nilly, each had a gourdful out of the pot.

Chapter 5

The Linders were all up and about the next morning, thanks to the dosing of herb tea, Mammy Linders said. Even the twins were as chirky as a couple of crickets. There was not a sneeze or a snuffle from either Jim or Joe.

But alas and alack for Step-Along! This morning the poor peddler had not only a terrible cold in his head, but he was nigh about doubled up with rheumatism.

"I didn't get hold of him soon enough; that's the trouble," Mammy declared. But she didn't give up, oh no, indeed. She made Step-Along a pallet right in front of the fire and started to brew more tea. She rubbed him well with goose grease salve, and she made a pine-tar plaster for his back.

Step-Along lay on his bed and groaned, not only with pain but worry. "I hate to be such a botheration to you all," he said.

"Foolishness and fiddlesticks!" Mammy scolded. "It's no botheration at all to help a body get well."

The others did their best to help. Susie went down the hollow, for more herbs had to be gathered to make a more strengthy tea. Joe and Jim gathered pine knots and kept a good fire

Susie went to gather more herbs

going. Pappy found time to play a fiddle tune now and then, just to cheer the peddler up and make him forget his troubles.

That night Step-Along was feeling much better. "By tomorrow," Step-Along declared, "I'll be able to go on my way to Far Beyant."

The Linders were glad to see their guest getting well in a hip-and-hurry.

Meanwhile, Susie had a notion. She talked it over with the twins. She asked Pappy's opinion and sought Mammy's approval. She asked them all not to say a single word about her notion. But she said no word to Step-Along of her surprise.

The peddler left his pallet bed and sat up to eat supper. They could see that he was better, for he ate a hearty meal. They gave him the rest of the company food from last night's supper.

The Linders had a bowl of corn mush apiece.

Pappy found time to play a fiddle tune now and then

After supper Step-Along was given the rocking chair in a corner where he would be out of the drafts and could stretch his long legs out to the bright, warm fire.

The peddler's keen eyes looked over every face glowing in the firelight. He might have been thinking that he ought to keep a still tongue in his head for manners' sake. Yet he understood the Linders' kind ways and, in turn, was planning a real surprise for all of them.

Pappy took down the fiddle and began to play a merry old jig. Such a gladsome tune it was that it sounded like happy laughter. Step-Along started to keep time with his hands and feet.

Susie began to hum the tune. Mammy caught up with her. The twins took up the song, singing turn and turn about:

A merry old jig

Joe:
> "Somebody stole my old coon dog,
>   I wish they'd bring him back;
> He'd run the big pigs over the fence,
>   The little ones through a crack."

Jim:
> "Somebody stole my old gray mule,
>   I hope he runs away;
> I'll ride him clear to Tucker Town,
>   And back again next day."

Joe:
> "Somebody stole my old red hen,
>   I wish they'd let her be;
> She laid a good egg every day,
>   On Sunday two or three!"

Jim:
> "Somebody stole my brindle cow,
>   I hope she jumps the fence;
> I wouldn't sell her for a dime,
>   Or even thirty cents!"

Step-Along was laughing so hard by the time this funny song ended that he lost his breath and choked on a chuckle. Mammy gave him a swig of tea, the twins thumped him on the back, and Susie opened the shutter of the one window of the cabin to let in a fresh air breeze.

Soon they had all settled down again. They started asking riddles. This turned out to be sure-enough fun. Step-Along knew one that nobody could guess.

> "Red in a house, red on a hill,
> If you feed it, live it will;
> Give it water, it will die;
> If you guess this, you're as smart as I!"

At last he had to tell them the answer: fire.

Pappy played another tune or so.

Mammy took the herb pot from the fire.

Then Susie brought another kettle and hung

Susie opened the shutter of the one window

it on the chimney hook. This was a part of her notion.

The twins stared knowingly and sniffed the air from time to time.

"What's in the kettle?" they asked her.

Susie smiled. "You'll know pretty soon!"

And pretty soon they did. A flavorsome fragrance filled the room. It was the sweet smell of sorghum molasses.

"It's a candy kettle!" the twins yelled, and they turned two or three somersaults just for the fun of it, glad at last they didn't have to keep quiet any more about Step-Along's surprise. Lazybones under the bed came out to caper around and sniff the good smell too.

Susie soon tested it with a drip in a gourdful of water. When the candy was done, it was taken from the fire. By and by when it was nearly cool, each had a portion of it poured into a saucer. It was eaten right away. The rest of the treat they pulled back and forth in well-greased fingers till it was stiff enough to cut into candy-sticks.

Step-Along said he would keep his candy-sticks to sweeten his trip tomorrow.

The merrymaking was over now, and everyone went to bed.

The sunball was peeking above the peak of Little Twin Mountain as Step-Along got ready for his journey-jaunt on the third day. He seemed to be feeling all right again.

"I'm as fine and fit as a fiddle-bow, strings and all," he added in mannerly fashion. "Thanks for all you've done for me."

Mammy Linders handed a poke of herbs to him. "Make yourself a mess o' tea the next time you are ailing."

The rest of the treat they pulled back and forth

Step-Along promised that he would.

Susie smiled over at the twins, and they smiled back at her. Here was one more brewing of Spring Tea which they wouldn't have to drink! Step-Along had saved them all from several extra dosings. Susie and the boys felt mighty-much obliged to him.

The peddler opened his shoulder pack to put the herb poke into it. But before he fastened it up, his hand went deep inside for certain things—certain fancy-fine treasures.

Step-Along searched out the faces of the family, as all eyes opened wide in delighted wonderment. "Here—here," he said happily. "A few little thank-gifts for you because you've all been so kind."

Out of the peddler's pack came a fine necktie for Pappy. For Mammy came the piece of dress goods, with buttons to match, and the pretty

The twins smiled back at her

lace. Next, he held out the two jackknives for the twins and then the shiny rattler for the baby. And last but not least, of all things—there were two red ribbons for Susie!

"So you'll have a bright bow apiece for your pigtails," Step-Along finished with a smile.

The Linders were so surprised they nearly forgot their manners. Then they remembered, for here were all the things they had admired two evenings ago. "Many thanks! Much obliged! Mighty much obliged!" they cried in a joyful, gladsome chorus. Even the baby yelled, "A-goo!" from his cradle by the hearth.

There were two red ribbons for Susie

More Books from The Good and the Beautiful Library!

Juddie
by Florence Whightman Rowland

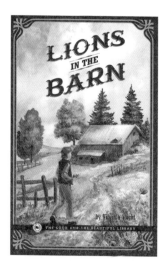

Lions in the Barn
by Virginia Voight

Over the Hills to Nugget
by Aileen Fisher

Zeke and the Fisher-Cat
by Virginia Frances Voight

www.thegoodandthebeautiful.com